Bad Hair Day

CATHERINE DOOLAN

• Pictures by Maeve Kelly •

THE O'BRIEN PRESS
DUBLIN

First published 2002 by The O'Brien Press Ltd,
20 Victoria Road, Dublin 6, Ireland.
Tel: +353 1 4923333; Fax: +353 1 4922777
E-mail: books@obrien.ie
Website: www.obrien.ie
Reprinted 2004.

ISBN: 0-86278-748-3

British Library Cataloguing-in-Publication
Doolan, Catherine
Bad hair day. - (O'Brien pandas ; 22)
1.Children's stories
I.Title II.Kelly, Maeve
823.9'2[J]

2   3   4   5   6   7   8   9   10
04   05   06   07   08   09

The O'Brien Press receives
assistance from

Typesetting, layout, editing, design: The O'Brien Press Ltd
Printing: Cox & Wyman Ltd

Can YOU spot the panda
hidden in the story?

Finn was not cool.
He wasn't sure what cool was,
but he knew he wasn't it.

His friends James and Ben
told him so every day.
'You're a nerd,' they said.

They said he was **un-cool**.
'Those football boots you have
are so un-cool,' they said.
'That bike of yours is
mega un-cool.'

Everything about Finn
seemed to be un-cool.

Finn was not happy.

The worst thing of all
was his hair.
Finn's hair was strange.

Sometimes it looked red
and sometimes
it looked orange.

It wasn't straight
and it wasn't curly.

But it was **thick**.
And there was **lots of it**.

'It's **monster** hair,'
said James and Ben.

Every bit of Finn's hair
seemed to have a mind
of its own.

It stood out in every direction,
and in the mornings
he did look a bit like
a monster.

Every morning
Mum got a wet cloth
and plopped it down
on his head.
'Yuck!' he said.

But it did make
his hair lie down.

It worked for about ten minutes, and then Finn's hair stood up again – for the whole day.

Finn's little sister Alva
was **born** cool.
She didn't even have to try.
She had blond hair that was
always straight and flat.

Mum never had to plop
a wet cloth on **her** head.

Everyone said Alva was cute.
When they said this
she always grinned at Finn
and he knew she was thinking:
And **you're not**.

It just wasn't fair.

'It's not fair, Mum,' Finn said.
'Why don't I have hair
like Alva's?'
But Mum said Finn's hair
was special.

'Dad's hair was
just like that
when he was a boy,'
she told Finn.
And she loved Dad's hair then –
and so did all the other girls!

Dad was bald now
so it was hard to think of him
with any hair at all!
Even Finn's new baby cousin
had more hair
than Dad had.

Anyway, Finn didn't want
girls loving his hair.
He just wanted to be cool.

When James and Ben
started to call him Freakhead,
and Mophead, and Frizzball,
and Steel Wool, that was **IT**.
Finn had had enough.

He knew he had to
do something.

He thought about it all day.

He thought about it in bed.

He could ask the hairdresser.
But she was a friend of Mum's –
and she knew exactly the way
Mum wanted his hair.

Nerdy.

No. He would have to
do something himself.

Then he thought about
Mum's own hair.
Mum loved her hair.

She had all sorts of stuff for it
in the bathroom.

And she put stuff on it
every few weeks
to keep it blond.

You see, Mum wasn't really
blond any more.
Her hair grew out brown.
Mum hated brown hair.

She rubbed this stuff
on her hair.

She left it on for a while.

When she washed it out again
it was **perfect**.

Finn had often seen her do it.
Surely it would work
for him too?

Finn raced to the bathroom.
It was full of all kinds of
hair goo.

There was stuff for
making your hair shiny.

Stuff for head lice – Yuck!

Stuff for greasy hair,
and stuff for dry hair.

There was even stuff
for normal hair.
He didn't need that anyway.
His hair was definitely
not normal.

There was, of course,
stuff for making your hair
blond.

The bathroom was
full of hair stuff.
Finn was thrilled.
Now, I'll sort out my hair,
he thought.

He ran down to the kitchen
and got a big bowl.
Mum used it for making scones.
It was perfect for his
special hair potion.

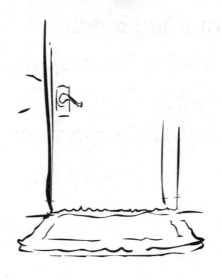

'What are you doing, Finn?'
called Mum.
'Eh ... nothing,' he said.
'I'm in the bathroom.'

Finn grabbed every bottle of
hair stuff he could find.

The stuff for greasy hair,
for dry hair,
even for normal hair.

He took the colour stuff
for the blond hair.

He didn't know
what some of the bottles
were for –
but he took them too.

He threw all the stuff
into the bowl.
He put in gel, hairspray
and shampoo as well.

It all made a
lovely brown mess
in the bowl.
It smelled very bad.
'Yuck!' he said.

Finn held his nose.

He closed his eyes.

He stuck his head
down into the **brown mess**.

He got his toothbrush
and rubbed the stuff
all over his hair.

Then he put a towel
around his head and waited,
just like Mum did.

He waited and waited.
He read a comic
to pass the time.

At last he decided it was ready.
He couldn't wait to see
his cool new look.

He took off the towel
to check his hair.
But where was his hair?

Finn's hair was **gone**.
He was nearly as bald as Dad.

There were bald patches
all over his head.

And where there was hair,
it was white or dirty yellow.

His head itched like mad.
There was a smell of
burnt rubber coming from it.

Finn stuck his head
under the cold tap.
More hair came off.

Finn was a sight!
And he was in
big trouble.

Finn started to howl.
Now James and Ben
would call him
even worse names.

How would he ever
go to school again?

Finn roared and screamed.
Mum and Dad came running.

Mum screamed too
when she saw the state of him.
'Your lovely hair,' she said.
What lovely hair? thought Finn.

Dad grabbed Finn
and put him in the car.
They went to the doctor.

The doctor was nice,
but she said it was
a very bad idea
to make hair potions.
They were very dangerous.
And they didn't work.

She put some soothing cream
on Finn's head
but it stuck to the little bits of
hair he still had.
It was a mess.

Dad whispered something
to the doctor.
She nodded.
Finn shook with fright.

What was going
to happen now?
Dad said he would **fix things**.

At home, Dad called
the hairdresser.
She came with all her stuff.

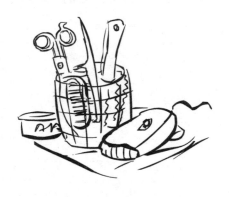

'Sorry, Finn, but this is
the best plan.
I'll have to give you
a **zero** blade,' she said.

Mum was in tears.
Dad tried to make a joke of it:
'We'll have two baldies
in the house now!' he said.

Mum cried even louder.
Alva just stared and stared.

The hairdresser shaved
Finn's head.

She shaved off
every bit of hair
that was left on it.

When she had finished
Finn was balder than Dad!

He was as bald as an egg.
And he was **not** happy.

Next day
Mum went to school with Finn
to tell the teacher
what had happened.

James and Ben
were sitting on the wall.
They stared at him.
Finn was nearly sick.
Now he really was a Freakhead.

'Hey!' shouted James.
Just look at **you**!'

Finn felt like running away.

'That is so cool,' said Ben.
'My Mum won't let me
get my head shaved.'

'What did your Dad say
when he saw it?' asked James.
'Was he mad?'
'No,' said Finn.
'Actually, it was **his** idea.'

Ben whistled.

'That is so cool,' he said again.

'My Dad is such a nerd.

He would never let me

get a zero blade.'

'Hey, Finn,' said James.
'Do you want
to play football with us?'

Finn could not believe it.
He was **cool** at last.

'No thanks,' he said,
and he smiled (coolly)
to himself.